DAVID LIVINGSTONE

Dan Larsen

Illustrated by
Ken Save

Uhrichsville, Ohio

ISBN 1-55748-259-4

Published by Barbour Publishing, Inc.
P.O. Box 719
Uhrichsville, Ohio 44683
http://www.barbourbooks.com

Printed in the United States of America.

CONTENTS

THIS LION... MUST DIE!

1

The Eyes of Death

The lion was about thirty yards away. It was as still as the flat rock it sat on. The hunter crouched behind a scraggly patch of bushes. Both barrels of his elephant gun were already cocked. This was closer than he had ever hoped to come to a lion in the wilds. But he had no choice now: This lion must die.

They had come out that morning, the great traveler and his native friends, the Bakhatla, to hunt the lions. For many days now the lions had closed in on Mabotsa, the tiny village in the valley. They had come down from the hills, lean and hungry, to take easy prey among the villagers' herds of cattle and sheep. Night and day, their roars boomed off the hills, echoing throughout the valley. In the first attack, one lion charged among the sheep, killing nine while the herd stood still, too terrified to move.

The Bakhatla, "the People of the Monkey," were as terrified as their sheep. "We are bewitched!" they would cry. "Who ever saw the lion, the lord of the night, kill our cattle by day?" The lion was a creature of the night, the Bakhatla knew. But these lions came boldly near the village in the heat of day, killing almost lazily, feeding only on some of the carcasses, while leaving others to bloat in the sun.

They must be stopped, said the great traveler, David Livingstone. The way to stop them, he knew, was to kill one and leave it lying in the field. The other lions would leave the area when they saw the dead one.

Today was the day of the hunt. David carried

"WE ARE BEWITCHED!"

his heavy-caliber double-barreled rifle. The native schoolmaster of the village, a man named Mebalwe, also had a gun. The other natives carried spears. The lions were on a small hill covered with trees. The Bakhatla encircled the hill and slowly closed in, beating the tall weeds with their spears and chanting to drive the lions to the waiting guns of Livingstone and Mebalwe. But, one by one, the lions broke through the ring of spearmen and disappeared into the fields. The Bakhatla were too frozen with fear to throw their spears. Soon they had covered the hill. The lions were gone.

All but one. It was huge, the biggest lion that Mebalwe had ever seen. He stiffened and then touched David on the shoulder and pointed. Now David could see the lion, barely. Its tawny hide was the same color as the parched ground.

DAVID COULD SEE THE LION...BARELY

This is the one, David thought. But he had to get closer. *Lord, give me courage,* he prayed silently. Then he cocked both barrels of his gun and crept forward. The natives must not see that he was too afraid to act, he knew. He must show them the way of courage. But he *was* afraid. Very afraid.

The lion was not looking at him. Slowly he stalked, hoping to come to a spare patch of bushes about thirty yards from the lion. His palms were sweaty now, his mouth dry. Step by step, he closed in. There was the bush, just ahead.

Then the lion turned and looked at him. David froze. And instantly he realized two things. One, the lion had known he was there, had known all along that he was coming. He saw this now in the lion's yellow eyes as they stared into his

DAVID FROZE !

own. And, two, the bush was no better than a cobweb between him and the lion. The glare from the lion's eyes seemed to burn a path straight through the flimsy branches.

No time to wait now. Shaking, David raised his rifle and squeezed both triggers. As if punched by a giant fist, the lion was punched backward off the rock.

David's knees were shaking. He couldn't see the lion behind the rock. But he had seen it go down. One of the Bakhatla now shouted, "He is shot! He is shot!" David took a deep breath. Then he began reloading his rifle.

Just as he was tamping a lead ball into a barrel, he thought he glimpsed, out of the corner of one eye, a lion's tail from behind the flat rock. The tail was stiff, pointing straight up. That's what a lion did with its tail, he knew, just

THE LION WAS PUNCHED BACKWARD...

before . . .

"The lion! The lion!" came the screams. David looked up. All he saw was a tan blur, all he heard was the snapping of the dry branches of the bushes, and all he felt was a sudden horrible pain in his left shoulder.

He realized he was on the ground several yards from where his rifle lay, the lion on top of him, its teeth in his shoulder. Those pale eyes were huge now, only inches from his face. They were as icy and full of death as a snake's. The lion's breath was like rotten meat.

David felt himself being shaken, like a rat in a dog's mouth. When the shaking stopped, the pain was gone. He felt nothing. His vision was blurred, and a sense of dreaminess, of floating, had come over him.

He didn't hear the rifle shots nor did he feel

THE LION WAS ON TOP OF HIM!

the lion let go of him. He didn't see it charge Mebalwe and clamp its teeth in his leg. Unknown to him, the bullets from his own gun, which had opened the lion's chest like an explosion, now finished their work, bleeding the last of the fierce life out of the beast. Finally the lion dropped in the dust and lay still.

His shoulder would never be the same. In time it would heal some, but his left arm would hang stiff for years. The bone was crunched into splinters. Eleven tooth marks left their scars.

But tonight in the village of Mabotsa, which means "A Marriage Feast," the Bakhatla held a celebration. Their white friend, their protector, had saved them. They would love him always, they swore. The feasting, laughing, and the stories of the day's hunt went on and on. But David Livingstone lay on soft grasses in a hut,

FINALLY... THE LION DROPPED IN THE DUST

tossing in fever, while a couple of the Bakhatla sponged him with cool water and prayed to his great God for his life.

Outside the village, the night was silent. There would be no roaring of the lions tonight. They would not come back, not to this place.

OUTSIDE...THE NIGHT WAS SILENT

WHERE NO MISSIONARY HAS EVER BEEN!

2

The Smoke of a Thousand Villages

David Livingstone had come to Mabotsa from the south. He had traveled hundreds of miles, through plains, across rivers, and over mountains. His way led north, always to the north. His life's work waited for him in the north, he knew. "There is a vast plain to the north," Robert Moffat, the great missionary to Africa, had told him. "I have sometimes seen, in the morning sun, the smoke of a thousand villages where no missionary has ever been."

Where no missionary has ever been! When David heard these words, he knew what lay ahead of him in life. He just knew. "I will go at once to Africa," he had said to Moffat.

Until he met Moffat, David hadn't known he would go to Africa. But he had long known he would be a missionary. He had heard the call as a boy.

He was born on March 19, 1813, in the village of Blantyre in Lanarkshire, Scotland. His father was a poor tea merchant. When David was ten he went to work in the Blantyre cotton mill. There he worked from six in the morning until eight in the evening. His job was to watch a cotton spinning frame and tie any threads of cotton that broke.

But though his body kept to the task, his mind was elsewhere. David had always wanted to learn new things. With half his first week's wages he bought a Latin grammar book. This he propped up at work by his spinner so he could read a sentence here and there while he

HE HAD HEARD THE CALL AS A BOY...

watched the cotton threads. Soon he also began to be tutored nights after work. Even after he left his teacher for the night, he would often stay up past midnight reading. His mother would have to take his books away and blow out his lamp.

His father, Neil Livingstone, was pleased to see that David, too, had a love of books and learning. He gave David history and travel books, classical works, and, most important to Neil Livingstone, the Bible.

But David's life was not all work and study. On weekends and holidays he would tramp for miles and miles all over the countryside. He grew strong and developed great stamina. He couldn't know it then, but all this was preparing him for his life's work.

At eighteen he was promoted to the position

HE GREW STRONG...

of spinner at the mill, a job that paid much better wages. David decided to save his money for the university. It would take many years but David was determined to study to become a doctor and a missionary.

David had read of a doctor missionary in China. Perhaps he too could go to China and be like that man. Like the Great Physician, Jesus Christ, who came to give life to all people, David longed to save lives in China.

He was accepted at the university in Glasgow, Scotland. One winter morning, he and his father began the long walk on the snowy road to Glasgow.

While at the university, David wrote a letter to the London Missionary Society offering himself as a missionary to China. The directors of the society told him they would accept

... AT THE UNIVERSITY, DAVID WROTE A LETTER

him if he went through a training course at a school in the little town of Chipping Ongar in Essex, near London, England.

At Ongar he met the man who would give him his life's vision. A tall, powerful man with a great bushy beard, Robert Moffat had just returned from Africa with stories of that huge, mysterious continent. Moffat told David of the "vast plain to the north" and the "smoke of a thousand villages where no missionary has ever been."

David knew he must go! He told the directors of the missionary society that he wished to go to Africa. They agreed to send him. Go to the north, they said, to this plain of a thousand villages where no missionary has yet been.

On the morning of November 17, 1840,

ROBERT MOFFAT HAD JUST RETURNED FROM AFRICA

twenty-seven-year-old David Livingstone hugged his father on the Broomielaw quay in Glasgow before walking up the gangway to his waiting ship, the *George*. They held each other a long time. Unable to speak out loud the words they felt, they said goodbye. They would never see each other again.

The ship *George* sailed around the Cape of Good Hope and into the bay of Algoa, where the Atlantic and Indian oceans meet. Here David landed and began the long journey inland.

They went on horseback and on foot, with an ox cart for their supplies. David's wanderings as a boy served him well now. He walked on and on tirelessly. Even the hardy African natives had trouble keeping up with him.

Isaac Taylor, a friend of David's at Chipping

THE SHIP SAILED INTO THE BAY OF ALGOA

Ongar, would many years later describe his walk: "I remember his step, the characteristic forward tread, firm, simple, resolute, neither fast nor slow, no hurry and no dawdle, but which evidently meant getting there." Another friend would write, "Fire, water, stone wall would not stop Livingstone."

Nothing would stop him now. The north, on to the north. On to the smoke of a thousand villages.

The days were blistering hot, the nights clear and cold. They slept under the stars and huddled in blankets around the ox cart in the early morning, warming fingers on tin cups of steaming black coffee. During the hottest time of the day, they would stop to rest sitting in the shade of the wagon.

They came to the village of Kuruman, where

NOTHING WOULD STOP HIM NOW!

Robert Moffat had lived. Moffat was now home in England on a visit. Kuruman had once been a dry, barren place, but now it was filled with fruit trees, vines, and gardens. Moffat had been a gardener before he became a missionary and he had used his skills here.

He dug ditches to bring water from the hillsides two miles away. Then he planted trees and gardens, using the water to irrigate. Kuruman was now a place of beauty and rest.

But David was not here to rest; he stayed only long enough to let the oxen recover. From Kuruman they went north to Lepelole. The people here called themselves the Bakwena, the "People of the Crocodile." David stayed here, waiting for word from the missionary society in London. Would they tell him to go on now, or wait here? Was this as far as he

PEOPLE OF THE CROCODILE!

would go?

He waited for six months. No one who spoke English was with him now. He wanted to learn the language and habits of these people.

The Bakwena men went out daily to hunt. The women and children stayed in the village, the women working, the children playing. They all spent their days in fear, though, of the village witch doctor. This doctor said he could "smell" witchcraft. He could tell, he said, if a person committed a crime. At his word, that person would be put to death.

David knew he had to free these people from their fear of witchcraft. He knew the only way to do this was to teach them about the one true God. So as he learned their language, he began to tell them about God. There is only one God, he said, one Father, who wanted the People of

HE BEGAN TO TELL THEM ABOUT GOD...

the Crocodile to be brothers, not enemies.

But David did not just talk. While in the village he noticed how dry the ground was. The witch doctor was said to be a rainmaker too. But despite his dances, charms, and prayers, no rain came. David said he would bring rain. With the only shovel in the village, one without a handle, he began to dig a canal from a nearby stream. Day by day, the men from the village began to dig with him using stones, knives, and even their hands. Soon there was a canal with many smaller ditches running from it into the gardens. Droopy vegetables lifted their heads and grew; grass began to sprout; flowers appeared.

The witch doctor laughed to see that this clever white traveler had done what all his gods could not. The Bakwena began to believe

HE BEGAN TO DIG A CANAL

it possible to be brothers after all. This great white traveler, who worked with his hands as well as his heart, must indeed serve a great God!

In the village of the Bakwena David started to build a house. But then the letter came. The missionary society said yes, go on to the north. Go beyond the places that other missionaries have gone before. Go to the land of the smoke from a thousand villages.

And this was the journey that took David to the People of the Monkey in the village of Mabotsa. And to the lion.

His journey would not end here. It had hardly begun. Yet before he could go on, he needed time to rest and to heal. And to build a school.

...THEN...THE LETTER CAME

THE TEACHER... WAS THE GREAT TRAVELLER

3

A Marriage Feast

The school had no desks, no chairs, and no pictures on the walls. The floor was the earth, the walls were mud brick, and the teacher was the great white traveler with the crippled left arm.

David Livingstone had now been in Africa for four years. He stayed here in the village of Mabotsa. The villagers helped him build a stone and brick house and they asked him to live with and be one of them and teach their children.

At first the children were afraid of the white man who killed the lion. He had a powerful God, they knew, a God who gave him strength and protected him. He seemed to fear nothing.

Why did he want the children to come to him in the schoolhouse? What would he do to them? They would not have come, but the Bakhatla chief and the schoolmaster Mebalwe said they must.

But on the first day of school, the children discovered that they had nothing to fear. The white schoolmaster was as gentle and kind as he was strong and brave. He sat on the ground with the children and spoke their language and learned their games. Sometimes he would cry as he told them of his great God. This God was everyone's God, the white teacher said, a God who loved the world so much that He came to earth to live as a man and to die as a man, so that anyone who believes in Him might live with Him forever.

David's days were very busy. He cut trees

...THEY HAD NOTHING TO FEAR

and made planks, built houses, gardened, taught in the school, doctored the sick and injured, and repaired guns and wagons and furniture and just about everything else. All the Bakhatla were his friends.

But David was lonely. He had no one to go home to at night, no one with whom to share his dreams and hopes and deepest thoughts.

One day he received glad news. His friend Robert Moffat was returning from England to the village of Kuruman. David set out on horseback to meet him. When he reached Kuruman, Moffat was not there yet. So after a day's rest, David rode south to met him. He went 150 miles before he saw Moffat's wagon coming up the road.

From a distance, David waved to his friend. As he came nearer he recognized Mrs. Moffat

DAVID SET OUT ON HORSEBACK

on the wagon bench. But sitting between Mr. and Mrs. Moffat was someone David didn't recognize, a young woman in a sunbonnet. David and Moffat shook hands in the road. He bowed to Mrs. Moffat, then to the young woman next to her.

"David, this is my eldest daughter, Mary," Robert said.

David mumbled hello. She smiled and then looked down at her hands in her lap.

"It has been a long time, my friend," said Moffat, his hand on David shoulder. "How are things in . . . David? David?"

David and Mary were soon engaged. David knew he had found the answer to his loneliness. It seemed perfect. The school in Mabotsa needed someone to teach the girls. Mary Moffat had been

"HOW ARE THINGS IN... DAVID... DAVID...?"

born in Africa and had spent many years there with her father. She knew the duties and hardships of missionary life. From the moment she saw him, she loved David Livingstone.

Before they could be married, though, there was much to do. David would have to return alone to Mabotsa to build a house for them. Meanwhile, he wrote to Colesburg, Africa, to get their marriage license, and he wrote to the mission directors in London, announcing his engagement and asking their approval for his plans for Mabotsa. He wanted to make the village a training center for missionaries from which students would be sent out into surrounding areas. This was what Moffat had done in Kuruman.

On August 1, 1844, during his journey north to Mabotsa, David wrote a letter to Mary.

"Whatever friendship we feel toward each

...SHE LOVED DAVID LIVINGSTONE

other," David wrote, "let us always look to Jesus as our common friend and guide, and may He shield you with his everlasting arms from every evil."

In Mabotsa David began building their house. Work left little time for him to think of Mary, waiting for him in Kuruman. But whenever he could, he would write to her. He sent this letter on September 12, 1844:

"I must tell you of the progress I have made. . . . The walls are nearly finished, although the dimensions are 52 feet by 20 outside, or about the same size as the house in which you now reside. I began with stone, but when it was breast-high, I was obliged to desist from my purpose to build it entirely of that material . . . . A stone falling . . . caught by me in its fall by the left hand, and it nearly broke my arm over

DAVID BEGAN BUILDING THEIR HOUSE

again. It swelled up again, and I fevered so much I was glad of a fire, although the weather was quite warm. I expected bursting and discharge, but Baba bound it up nicely, and a few days' rest put all to rights. . . . six days have brought the walls up a little more than six feet.

"The walls will be finished long before you receive this, and I suppose the roof too, but I have still the wood of the roof to seek. It is not, however, far off . . . .

"You must excuse soiled paper; my hands won't wash clean after dabbling mud all day. And although the above does not contain evidence of it, you are as dear to me as ever, and will be as long as our lives are spared. I am still your most affectionate

D. Livingstone."

"...IT NEARLY BROKE MY ARM OVER AGAIN"

David also wrote Mary something of life in Mabotsa. In October, 1844, he wrote:

"All goes on pretty well here; the school is sometimes well, sometimes ill attended. I had a great objection to school-keeping, but I find in that as in almost everything else I set myself to as a matter of duty, I soon become enamored of it. A boy came three times last week, and on the third time could act as monitor to the rest through a great portion of the alphabet. He is a real Makhatla, but I have lost sight of him again. If I get them on a little, I shall translate some of your infant-school hymns into Sichuana rhyme, and you may yet, if you have time, teach the tunes to them. I, poor mortal, am as mute as a fish in regard to singing . . . .

"And now I must again, my dear, dear Mary,

DAVID WROTE MARY OF LIFE IN MALBOTSA

bid you good-bye. Accept my expressions as literally true when I say, I am your most affectionate and still confiding lover,

D. Livingstone."

The house was soon finished, the marriage licenses came from Colesburg, and Mary came from Kuruman. Then in the village of "A Marriage Feast," there was indeed a marriage feast.

... THERE WAS INDEED A MARRIAGE FEAST!

"DO STAY... PLEASE..."

4

The Land of Many Rivers

In Mabotsa the Bakhatla had all gathered in the little village road. They had not gathered today to celebrate, but to mourn, to say good-bye. The wagon was loaded, the oxen were harnessed, and the horses were saddled. The white traveler and his wife were ready.

Some of the Bakhatla came up to the Livingstones and said, "Do stay, please. We will build another house for you." They must go north, Livingstone said. Not too long ago another missionary had settled in Mabotsa and David and Mary felt the time had come to move on. They, too, were sorry to leave their friends, the Bakhatla. But they wanted more than anything to be obedient to God and to go where He led them.

They came to the village of Chonuane, forty miles to the north. In Chonuane there lived the Bakwena, "the People of the Crocodile." The chief, Sechele, welcomed them with great kindness. Here Livingstone built another stone house for Mary and himself and a school. Here the Livingstones had their first child, a boy. They named him Robert, after Mary's father.

But they would not stay here long. Chonuane was a dry place: There were no streams or lakes and one summer, month after month, there was no rain. The Livingstones would have to move on, David told the Bakwena. Then they would move with the Livingstones, the Bakwena told David.

And one morning everyone in the village, with all their possessions in carts and on their backs,

THE LIVINGSTONES HAD THEIR FIRST CHILD

started northward with David and Mary and little Robert.

They found a place to build another village by a river. They called this place Kolobeng. Here David, with the help of Chief Sechele, built another house for Mary and himself and yet another school. They dug ditches from the river into the villagers' gardens. The Livingstones were as busy as ever, David teaching the boys and preaching, building, fixing, and doctoring, Mary teaching the girls and taking care of baby Robert and their household.

They stayed here for several years. Mary had two more children, a boy, Thomas, and a girl, Agnes. They wondered how long this would be their home.

One day some messengers came to the village. They were from Chief Lechulatebe, they said,

...HOW LONG WOULD THIS BE THEIR HOME?

who lived by a great lake that lay hundreds of miles to the north on the other side of the Kalahari Desert. Lechulatebe had heard somehow of David Livingstone, the messengers said. Would the great traveler come north with them to see their chief?

David had heard of a lake across the Kalahari. Was this his destiny, the land of the "smoke of a thousand villages?" Now he would find out.

The river at Kolobeng was getting low. The rain had not come for months. Some of the Bakwena were grumbling that David's God could not bring rain. David wished to find a place with plenty of water. Perhaps these messengers from Chief Lechulatebe brought the answer to this wish.

With three other travelers, Mr. Murray, Mr. Oswell the hunter, and Colonel Steele, David set

WAS THIS HIS DESTINY?

out with the messengers. They went over wooded hills and down into the bed of a wide river, long dry. They followed the riverbed northward. The country here was flat with thorny trees. Antelope grazed in the grasses. Monkeys climbed in the trees. At night lions roared in the darkness.

But as they went, the ground became more and more sandy. The oxen went slower and slower as the wagon wheels sank deeper and deeper. The sun was scorching in the deep blue sky; they found no water.

At last they reached Lake Ngami, the home of Chief Lechulatebe. David and his three friends were the first white men ever to see this lake. It was huge, stretching beyond their sight. Here David learned of a land farther to the north, "full of rivers—so many that no one can tell their number—and full of trees."

...HUGE... STRETCHING BEYOND THEIR SIGHT

David decided he must return for Mary and their children. Together they would cross Lake Ngami to find this land of rivers.

When they went back, Kolobeng was drier than ever. Mary and the children had moved to a hut nearer the river, now only a muddy trickle. Livingstone was convinced they could not live here in the desert of the south. They must go north.

They went in a caravan of eighty cattle and twenty men on horseback. Mary and the children rode in one of the wagons.

They would eventually reach Lake Ngami, but not on this journey. This time they would get only so far as the Zouga River. As they rested there, many of the traveling party became ill. David and Mary's own children tossed in fever for days. Finally David decided to return south

DAVID AND MARY'S CHILDREN TOSSED IN FEVER

to the drier air of the desert. The air there, he knew, was healthier to breathe.

Their children recovered, months later they set out again. This journey did take them to the lake. David and Mary stood on the shore and laughed as their three little children paddled and splashed in the cool water.

They would not go farther north to find the land of many rivers, not this time. The Livingstone children again became ill. They had to go back.

They tried again almost two years after David's first journey to Lake Ngami. But this time there was no water. Even the underground streams, which the natives knew how to find, were dried up. An accident with the wagon carrying their water barrels cost them all the water they had brought. For four days they went without water.

Of all the caravan, David suffered the worst.

THEY HAD TO GO BACK

His agony was in hearing the parched little voices of his children as they cried for water. He suffered even more as he saw the pain and fear in his wife's eyes. He knew she was struggling to be brave and cheerful. When he looked into her eyes, he saw not blame or bitterness, only love. He would later write of this time.

"The next morning , the less there was of water the more thirsty the little rogues became. The idea of their perishing before our eyes was terrible. It would almost have been a relief to me to have been reproached with being the entire cause of the catastrophe, but not one syllable of upbraiding was uttered by their mother, though the tearful eye told the agony within. In the afternoon of the fifth day, to our inexpressible relief, some of the men returned with a supply of that fluid of which we had never before felt

HE SUFFERED AS HE SAW THE PAIN

the true value."

At last they reached the lake! Now David could look into his wife's eyes and see only relief, not dread.

On the shore of the lake, David met another chief from farther north. This chief's name was Sebituane. He was a powerful chief with a large tribe. In his travels David had heard of this chief and he eagerly accepted Sebituane's invitation to come north with him to his village in the land of the lakes.

They traveled eastward around Lake Ngami. Farther north they came to a wide river. David discovered that this river, the Zambezi, which flowed into the Indian Ocean, could be a way into Central Africa from the coast. No one had ever visited this part of the African continent.

As they rode the gentle waves in canoes, David

SEBITUANE...WAS A POWERFUL CHIEF

saw a vision. Missionaries and traders could come in from the east or west coast. The missionaries could build schools in the villages and teach these people about Jesus Christ, who died for them. They could teach the people new trades and skills. Some of the villages were so poor that children starved to death.

As they continued northward, David learned of another reason to open up a way into Central Africa: *slavery*. Sometimes slave traders bought children from poor natives; sometimes villages were raided. Old people were murdered, huts were burned, and children were snatched away from their families and herded to the coast in chains. Many died of starvation and some died of heartache on the journey.

David burned inside at the thought of slavery. He would find a way to open up Central Africa,

SLAVERY!

build missionary training centers and schools, and unite the peoples against the slave trade. A way to the coast would allow these people to trade their ivory, coffee, and cotton—and not their children.

Much exploration of this area would be needed. But that would have to wait. David's children became sick again and again as they traveled through this humid, swampy area. The air was healthier in the desert to the south, but there was no water there. With his heart breaking, he realized there was only one answer: Mary and the children must return to England while he and his three friends explored farther to the north, to find an area where they could build a home. It had to be a high, dry land with a good supply of water—a lake or a large river. When he was finished with their house, David would send for

MARY AND THE CHILDREN MUST RETURN TO ENGLAND

his family. There they build a missionary training center. There he and Mary could raise their family. Their travels would be over.

But now a very long journey lay ahead of them. They turned south once again, this time to go all the way back to Cape Town on the southern coast. There they would say goodbye—for a while.

THEY TURNED SOUTH ONCE AGAIN

"MY DEAREST MARY... HOW I MISS YOU"

5

Alone Again

Livingstone guessed he would need two years. That would be enough time to find a good spot and build their home. It would be the longest two years of his life! (He didn't know that it would turn out to be almost five.) Before he left Cape Town he wrote a letter to his wife.

"My Dearest Mary,

"How I miss you now and the dear children! . . . I see no face now to be compared with the sunburnt one which has so often greeted me with its kind looks. . . . Take the children all around you and kiss them for me. Tell them I have left them for the love of Jesus, and they must love Him too, and avoid sin, for that displeases Jesus. I shall be delighted to hear of you all safe in England. . . ."

David also wrote to his daughter Agnes who was then four years old.

"My Dear Agnes,

"This is your own little letter. Mamma will read it to you and you will hear her just as if I were speaking to you. . . .

"I am still at Cape Town. You know you left me there when you all went into the big ship and sailed away. Well, I shall leave Cape Town soon. Malatsi has gone for the oxen, and then I shall go away back to Sebituane's country, and see Seipone and Meriye, who gave you the beads and fed you with milk and honey.

"I shall not see you again for a long time, and I am very sorry. I have given you back to Jesus, your Friend—your Papa who is in

"...MAMA WILL READ IT TO YOU"

heaven."

A few days later David climbed into the ox cart and started on the long journey north.

He stopped at Kuruman to see the Moffats, and they gave him discouraging news. A band of slave-trading Boers had raided Chief Sechele's village of Kolobeng. They had shot many of Sechele's people, the Bakwena, and had stolen all their cattle. They had even broken into the house that David and Mary had lived in and taken the furniture and torn up all his books and destroyed his medicines.

Staying with the Moffats was Masebele, the wife of Sechele. She had escaped the village with her baby. Sechele had also escaped, she said, but they had not been together and she did not know where he went.

"I hid in a cleft in the rock, with this little

THEY SHOT MANY OF SECHEL'S PEOPLE

baby," she said. She sat rocking the baby, who was asleep. "The Boers came closer and closer, shooting with their guns. They came till they were on the rock just above my head. I could see the muzzles of the guns above the clefts as they fired. The baby began to scream and I felt sure that they would hear us and capture us, but I took off these armlets and gave them to baby to play with. That kept baby quiet and the Boers passed on without finding us."

"The Boers have made up their minds to close the country," David now wrote to his wife. "I am determined to open it. Time will show who will win. I will open a path through the country— or PERISH."

They went north again, across the great Kalahari Desert. By day they saw herds of antelope and

"I HID IN A CLEFT... IN THE ROCK..."

buffalo. They saw the ostrich and the cheetah streaking through the dry grasses. By night they heard the lions pacing and snarling all around their camp.

They came to a wide river, too deep for the wagons. They paddled across the river on a raft to a wide, marshy grassland. Here the water was ankle deep and the grasses knee high. They had to leave the raft and wade.

The grass was rough and very sharp. It bit into the men's legs as they waded. David's pant were soon torn out at the knees. He cut his handkerchief in two and wrapped his knees with the pieces.

They soon came to deeper water. This was too deep to wade in. The grasses grew so thick here that they would have to cut their way. One of the men shouted and pointed. There

THEY SAW HERDS OF ANTELOPES

was a path where the grasses had been trampled into the water, probably by a hippopotamus. They could swim through here, the man said. No, look! another said. There were snakes swimming in the water. Their bite was deadly.

They saw some trees in the distance and when they arrived there a couple of the men climbed the trees to scout the land.

"Look, there is deeper water down river!" one of the men shouted. "I think our raft can pass through there."

They let the raft float downstream to the deeper water and began to paddle through. The mosquitoes were thick in the hot, humid afternoon air. The men paddling had to stop often and swat at their sweaty arms and legs. At times the water was too shallow to paddle in and the men would have to jump off the raft

"...OUR RAFT CAN PASS THROUGH HERE!"

and push. Their shoulders and backs ached, and the sweat dripped off their noses and stung their eyes.

They came to thicker grasses again. But the water was too shallow for paddling so they had to go on and on downstream, looking for a way through the grasses. The afternoon passed and evening came. They still had not found a way through.

As the sun was dropping under the horizon, the men saw a village on the north bank, behind them. They decided to paddle back across the river and see if they could stay there tonight.

They pulled the raft onto the bank and climbed up a low hill into the village. As they neared the first huts, Livingstone stopped suddenly and stared. Then he threw his head back and

THE MEN WOULD JUMP OFF THE RAFT AND PUSH

laughed. These were friends! He recognized them as some of Sebituane's people, the Makololo. He had met them on his last journey with his family.

Now cries of joy came from the darkening streets. "Livingstone! Our friend!"

A man came up to David and cried as the two of them embraced. Then the man stood back, laughing. "He has dropped among us from the clouds," he said, "yet came riding on the back of a hippopotamus. We Makololo thought no one could cross the Chobe River without our knowledge, but here he drops among us like a bird."

That night they sat under the stars with their Makololo friends and they ate and talked and laughed. The next day, the travelers and many of the Makololo went back to the raft. The

THE MAN STOOD BACK... LAUGHING!

Makololo took the wagons apart and brought them, piece by piece, back to the village. They drove the oxen into the river, making them swim to the other side. The Makololo knew the ways though the grasses to the south bank. They took the wagons and the oxen to this bank and there they put the wagons back together.

In a few days the Makololo took David and his men to the capital of the Makololo, a village call Linyanti, where 6000 Makololo lived. Here, too, lived Sekeletu, the son of Sebituane, whom David had met on his last journey. David and Sebituane had become close friends in the few weeks they spent together, but, sadly, Sebituane caught fever and died. Now Sekeletu ruled in his place. He was as kind as his father had been.

The two now met in the village street and

SEBITUANE WAS AS KIND AS HIS FATHER

Sekeletu brought David to his hut. They gave each other gifts and they talked of Sebituane and of the slave traders and of David's work in Sekeletu's country.

David and his men stayed here for a few weeks. Sekeletu quickly grew to love David. He began to call him "my new father." They sat together one morning by Sekeletu's fire, drinking coffee and talking. Sekeletu smiled. "Your coffee tastes better than that of the traders," he said, "because they like my ivory, but you like me."

At night David, standing on a wagon, read his Bible to the Makololo. In silence the people would shake their heads in wonder as they heard the stories of Jesus and His followers.

During their talks David told Sekeletu of his desire to open a road from the coast into the

...DAVID...STANDING ON A WAGON...READ HIS BIBLE

center of the country. Up this road missionaries and doctors and teachers could come; down this road the African people could carry their ivory and cotton and coffee to the coast where they could sell them. This would open up the country, David said, and would do away with the slave trade.

"I like this vision," Sekeletu said. He was beaming. Later, he called a gathering of the village leaders and told them of David's plans.

Sekeletu wanted to send men with David to guide him in his quest. Some of the leaders said no. "Where is the white doctor taking you?" asked one old man. "He is throwing you away! Your garments already smell of blood!" But others said yes. They would not agree to help just anyone, they said. But this man had earned their respect and their love. He was not

"YOUR GARMENTS ALREADY SMELL OF BLOOD!"

like the traders who came through the village, they said. He wanted nothing for himself. He wanted only to help these people and to stop the horrible slave trade. If he would serve them, then they would serve him, and, yes, even die for him.

They came to David late that night, Sekeletu and three of his chiefs. Sekeletu was smiling. "Yes, my new father," he said. "We will help you. We will go with you wherever you wish to go."

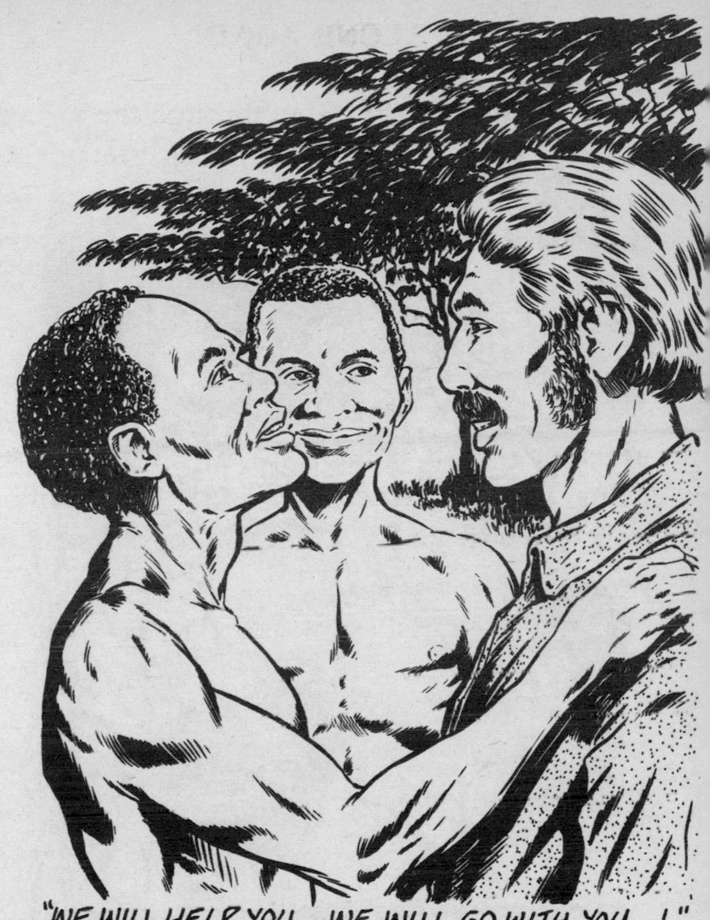

"WE WILL HELP YOU... WE WILL GO WITH YOU...!"

"THE NJAMBI ARE COMING!"

6

The Long Trail

The cry went throughout the camp. "The Njambi are coming!"

Carrying swords and spears, faces streaked with war paint, the Njambi came. In the camp the Makololo scattered about, grabbing their spears and rifles, yelling to one another, crying out to their gods for protection.

The great white traveler remained seated on his camp stool. He held his double-barreled rifle across his knees.

Off in the forest the drums were growing louder and louder. A warrior stepped out from the trees into the camp, his face in a fierce scowl. "The chief must have a man, an ox, a gun, powder, some cloth, or a shell. If not, you must go back. Or die."

David shook his head. "Tell the chief—" Just then the chief stepped into the clearing. Behind him came several warriors carrying spears, all pointed at David on his stool. The warriors began nodding to one another and gesturing with their spears toward David. Behind David, the Makololo were crouched, aiming their rifles at the strange warriors, holding up their spears, ready to spring.

Now the chief barked, "You heard my payment. I must have a man, an ox, a gun, powder, cloth, or a shell or you go back. Or die."

The men on both sides were murmuring now. The murmur rose to a clamor.

"Be seated," David said. There was no fear in that voice. It was quiet and steady. Sud-

THERE WAS NO FEAR IN THAT VOICE

denly everyone was silent, tensed. *Would the strangers attack?* the Makololo wondered. *Would their chief strike down this white man?* the Njambi wondered.

The chief, his eyes fixed on David's face, slowly sat down. His warriors stared at one another.

"Why do you ask me to pay to walk on the ground of God, our common Father?" David asked calmly,

The chief did not answer. To this question he had no answer. All the peoples of Africa called all the land "common." They believed it was God's, not theirs.

But for some tribes, things had changed. The slave trade—the raiding, destroying, and the murdering—had turned these peoples bitter. They were once friendly and trusting; now

THE CHIEF SLOWLY SAT DOWN

they were suspicious of everybody. They had become greedy. They demanded payment of anyone who wished to travel through their land. Especially they wanted "man," *slaves.* This, too, they had learned from the slave traders.

The chief of the Njambi ignored David's question. He threw his chin up. "You must give me man," he said. "Man or go back."

"Never," David said "I will die before I give one of my brothers into slavery." He stood up and went into his tent. Then he came out carrying several bundles. He offered the chief a shirt. The chief said no. He added beads. The chief shook his head. He added a large handkerchief. The chief growled, then said again that he wanted man.

His warriors had again stirred themselves

"NEVER!!"

into a frenzy. One of them now whooped shrilly and charged at David, his sword raised.

David did not flinch. Just as the warrior came within reach, he whipped his rifle up and stuck the barrel on the man's chin.

The man shrieked and ran into the forest, Slowly, David lowered his rifle. His eyes were on the chief, still sitting on the ground. "We will not strike the first blow," David said "If you do, the guilt of blood is on your head."

The chief's warriors all held their spears ready. The Makalolo, too, were ready. The chief saw the look on David's face. He saw the spears and guns of the Makololo aimed at him and his men. Then he looked down at his hands. They relaxed their grip on the spear. He stood up and bowed slightly to

...HE WHIPPED HIS RIFLE UP!

David. "You may pass," he said quietly, Then he and his warriors disappeared into the forest.

Twenty-seven young Makololo men had gone with David. They set out for the Zambezi River to the north. David had decided to travel up the Zambezi until it turned to the east. They would then leave the Zambezi and strike westward on the Kassai River, then northwest across the Kwango River to the Lucalla River. Then it would be due west on to Loanda on the coast.

At first things went well. But as they passed out of the lands of Chief Sekeletu, they began to have trouble with some of the tribes who were not friendly to travelers. They had not had to fight, not yet, but they had come close, as with the Njambi.

SOME OF THE TRIBES WERE NOT FRIENDLY...

"Man, ox, gun, or tusk you must give me," each chief would say, or David and his men would not be able to pass through. "Man" David would never give; "ox" he could hardly spare; "gun" he had only enough of for themselves, for hunting; "tusk" he had, but he hated to part with these. They were from Sekeletu who sent them with David so he could begin trade for Sekeletu's people on reaching Loanda.

They had over 1500 miles to go to reach the coast. They had to cross streams and pass through flat, scorched lands. At times they went through forests so thick that they had to chop down trees so the wagons could pass through. This was slow, painful work. David was almost constantly ill with the African fever now. It weakened him so much that he

MAN... DAVID WOULD NEVER GIVE!

could barely hold himself up while riding his ox. The fever burned in him day after day, week after week. He grew thinner and thinner. Many times he was delirious and lay in his tent tossing and moaning, bathed in sweat.

His Makololo friends became worried for him. They had grown to love him on this journey. He had proved himself to be a true brother to them. They knew he would give his life for them; and they swore they would give theirs for him.

Then the rains came. Day after day, rain dripped from the leaves and the hanging vines onto their heads as they passed through forests, and it poured on them as they crossed grassy plains and streams. Even their canvas tents became soaked through. At night the rain would drip in their faces as they slept

HIS MAKOLOLO FRIENDS GREW WORRIED FOR HIM

in their wet blankets. Their clothes became moldy and clung to their raw skin.

In some of the villages they passed through the people whispered to the Makololo that David Livingstone was leading them to their deaths. Tired and homesick and soaked from the rains, the Makololo began to wonder. *Was it true? Where were they going?*

David saw the change in his friends. They were growing more silent and sullen, more disheartened. Would they abandon him? Could he even blame them if they did?

One night David sat huddled in a wet blanket around a sputtering, hissing fire with several of the Makololo. The rain dripped steadily from the tree branches overhead. The fire would soon be out, it seemed, and there was no more dry wood anywhere. Earlier

DAVID SAT HUDDLED IN A WET BLANKET...

that day some of the men had come to him and threatened to return. "If you go back, still I shall go on," he had said. Now he left the fire and crawled into his wet tent and lay there shivering with fever. He had never felt so alone, so lost, so hopeless.

As he lay there he thought of his dear Mary and their children. He wondered what their lives were like now in England, without him. As he wondered when he would see them again, his tears flowed down his weatherbeaten cheeks.

The flap to his tent opened, and one of his closest Makololo friends, Mohorisi, crawled to him. He reached out and gently touched David's cheek.

"We will never leave you," Mohorisi said, his voice shaking.

"WE WILL NEVER LEAVE YOU"

Then there were two, three, four men in the tent. They, too, were sobbing gently. "We are your children," they said. "We will die for you. We spoke in bitterness before. We will not leave you. You will see what we can do!"

"WE WILL DIE FOR YOU"

"...THE WORLD SAID TO US... I AM FINISHED..."

7

And Back Again

They came out onto a high plain and there below them was the sea, sparkling in the sun. The Makololo had never seen the sea. They stood now without moving or speaking, simply staring at the water.

"We marched along with our father," one of them would later say, "believing that what the ancients had always told us was true, that the world has no end; but all at once the world said to us, 'I am finished; there is no more of me!' "

The journey had taken over six months. David had suffered again and again from the African fever. Now walking into the streets of Loanda, he was bone thin.

They stayed here for several weeks. The Makololo got jobs unloading a coal ship. David became friends with the captain, a British man. "You have worked and traveled without rest for fourteen years," the captain said. "You are ill. Come home with us and rest—come see your wife and daughter and your sons again. All Britain will cheer to see you."

David wanted badly to go home. But he was responsible for twenty-seven young men who had come 1500 miles with him and pledged their lives to him. He could not just leave them here. No, he told the captain, he would have to take the Makololo back. They were far from home and would never find their way back without him. David had learned navigation skills from a ship captain, and he used these to find his way across Africa. He must guide

HE WOULD HAVE TO TAKE THE MAKOLOLO BACK

his men home.

But he did send his journal home. In all his travels he had written of places, people, the land, the rivers, the mountains—and the slave trade. His information would later prove valuable to the world in understanding much of the land then called "the Dark Continent." His written accounts would do much to stop slavery in the world.

They started back to Linyanti. David had a new canvas tent as a gift from the British captain. The Makololo carried, bundled in their packs, new striped European suits and bright red caps, gifts from the sailors on the captain's ship. David carried everything he owned in four tin canisters, each about fifteen inches square. One held shirts, pants, and

THEY STARTED BACK TO LINYANTI

shoes; the second, medicines; the third, books; and the fourth, a lantern. Whenever they passed through villages, he would light this lantern at night, hang it from a wagon, and preach to the natives. They would stare fascinated at the lantern while David spoke of the light that came into the world. The darkness is passing away, he would say, and the real light is already shining: God is light, he would say, and there is no darkness in Him at all And his listeners would wonder about this God, who called people to walk in light and not in darkness.

As David and his Makololo friends journeyed westward, they saw more and more darkness. In the villages where they rested, the slavers would sometimes lead captives through the streets, captives from other tribes and other

THE SLAVERS WOULD LEAD CAPTIVES THROUGH THE STREETS

lands. Men, women, and children were herded like cattle, chained one to another with forked poles on their necks and iron hands on their wrists. David saw that many of the wrist bands dangled empty, and he knew why they were empty. In his journeys he would many times pass by the bodies of people who had died as they walked in these chains and had been thrown to the side of the path. Many had died of starvation or thirst, but many more died for another reason.

"It is brokenheartedness of which the slaves die," David would later write in his journal. "Even children, who showed wonderful endurance in keeping up with the chained gangs, would sometimes hear the sound of dancing and the merry tinkle of drums in passing near a village: then the memory of home and happy

HE WOULD...MANY TIMES...PASS THE BODIES OF PEOPLE

days proved too much for them, they cried and sobbed, the broken heart came on, and they rapidly sank."

He had already determined to destroy the slave trade. A few years earlier, while in Cape Town after seeing his family off to England, he had written a letter to the mission directors in London telling them of his hope.

"Consider the multitudes that in the Providence of God have been brought to light in the country of Sebituane; the probability that in our efforts to evangelize we shall put a stop to the slave trade in a large region, and by means of the highway into the north which we have discovered bring unknown nations into the sympathies of the Christian world. . . . Nothing but a strong conviction that the step will lead to the Glory of Christ would make me orphanize

...HE HAD DETERMINED TO DESTROY THE SLAVE TRADE

my children. . . . Should you not feel yourselves justified in incurring the expense of their support in England, I shall feel called upon to renounce the hope of carrying the Gospel into that country. . . . But stay, I am not sure; so powerfully convinced am I that it is the will of our Lord that I should go, I will go, no matter who opposes; but from you I expect nothing but encouragement."

From the directors he got nothing but encouragement. "The Directors of the London Missionary Society signified their cordial approval of my project by leaving the matter entirely to my own discretion," he wrote, "And I have much pleasure in acknowledging my obligations to the gentlemen composing that body for always acting in an enlightened spirit, and with as much liberality as their constitution would

"... IT IS THE WILL OF OUR LORD... I SHOULD GO"

allow."

The slave trade was but one darkness; witchcraft was another. The witch doctors killed as many of their own people as the slavers ever did. The witch doctors would make accused people drink poison to prove their innocence or guilt. If the person died, he was guilty, the witch doctors said. If he lived, he was innocent. The people in the villages lived in fear of their witch doctor. To disobey his law was death, they believed.

David told the people not to fear the witch doctors. The poison is what kills, he told them, not the witch doctors' magic. Do not walk in darkness, in fear, he told them, but believe in Jesus Christ, who came to set people free from fear and darkness and death.

Despite the darkness in this land, David vowed

THE PEOPLE LIVED IN FEAR OF THE WITCH DOCTOR

to fight the darkness with the light.

They came into Libonta, the first village of Chief Sekeletu, as heroes. Everyone in the village came out into the streets to cheer David and his twenty-seven men. He had kept his word. He had safely brought the twenty-seven back to their home. They held a day of thanksgiving on July 23, 1855.

"The men decked themselves out in their best," David wrote in his journal, "for all had managed to preserve their suits of European clothing, which, with their white and red caps, gave them a rather dashing appearance. They tried to walk like soldiers, and called themselves 'my braves.' Having been again saluted with salvos from the women, we met the whole population, and having given an address on

...GAVE THEM A RATHER DASHING APPEARANCE

divine things, I told them we had come that day to thank God before them all for His mercy in preserving us from dangers, from strange tribes and sicknesses. We had another service in the afternoon. They gave us two fine oxen to slaughter, and the women have supplied us abundantly with milk and meal. This is all gratuitous, and I feel ashamed that I can make no return. My men explain the whole expenditure on the way hither, and they remark gratefully: 'It does not matter, you have opened a path for us, and we shall have sleep.' Strangers from a distance come flocking to see me, and seldom come empty-handed. I distribute all presents among my men."

They went on to Linyanti. Sekeletu welcomed David as his own father. He was excited to hear that David had found a way to the west

"THE WOMEN SUPPLIED US ABUNDANTLY"

coast.

"But it is a long, hard way," David said. And he now wondered if a better way was to travel along the Zambezi River to the east coast.

"We shall try," Sekeletu said. This time Sekeletu would send a 120 men, along with oxen for riding and for food.

This time when they set out Sekeletu himself went with David. They traveled down the Chobe River to where it met the Zambezi River. Some paddled canoes while others drove the oxen along the bank.

Thunder was booming in the night sky as they came to a thick forest. Just as they passed through the first trees, rain came. David was on land with a small band of the Makololo. The others had drifted down river in the canoes

THUNDER WAS BOOMING IN THE NIGHT SKY

The tents and most of the blankets were in the canoes. The men in the forest had only a few blankets and supplies; they would have to sleep without a tent tonight. It was pitch dark among the trees now. Lightning arced across the sky in wide bands and in these brief flashes the men picked their way deeper and deeper into the forest. They found a tall tree with thick foliage and lay down under it. They were soaked and shivering and aching.

David lay hugging his knees, his teeth chattering. Suddenly he felt a hand touch his shoulder. He looked up but could see no one. Then two strong hands draped a blanket over him and Sekeletu's voice said, "Here, my father, is my blanket. You take it to keep you warm."

David tried to refuse, but Sekeletu tucked the blanket around his feet and back. "You must,"

TWO STRONG HANDS DRAPED A BLANKET OVER HIM

Sekeletu said, and then he went off under another tree and lay down to sleep in the rain.

It was March 3, 1856. They had come into Tette, an inland Portuguese station on the Zambezi River. They were about 300 miles from the coast, but David could go no farther without a rest. The fever plagued him day after day until he was so weak he couldn't walk. The Makololo had to carry him on a litter made of branches.

A commander in the Portuguese army stationed in Tette took David into his home. Here he rested, too weak to travel, until 23 March.

When he was well enough, David went by canoe down the Zambezi to the east coast. He was going home. He had settled his Makololo

THE MAKOLOLO HAD TO CARRY HIM

friends on plantations in Tette where they could work and earn wages until his return.

From the port city of Quilimane he boarded a ship bound for England. He had not seen his country for sixteen years, or his own wife and children for five years.

He knew he would return. "Nothing but death will prevent my return," he had told the Makololo. But now he needed a rest. A long rest.

HE NEEDED A REST... A LONG REST

HIS LETTER CAME...HE WAS COMING HOME

8

Home

The last five years had been hard for Mary Livingstone. Alone in England with her four children, sometimes not hearing news of her husband for long periods of time, she began to break down under the strain. But she also began to pray more and more. As she continued to pray, she began to feel peace, knowing that her Lord was able to take care of her husband, even if she could not. And then his letter came. David was coming home!

At the port of Southampton, David read the poem that Mary had written to him when she got his letter:

A hundred thousand welcomes,

and it's time for you to come
From the far land of the foreigner, to your country and your home.
O long as we were parted, ever since you went away,
I never passed a dreamless night, or knew an easy day.
Do you think I would reproach you with the sorrows that I bore?
Since the sorrow is all over, now I have you here once more,
And there's nothing but the gladness and the love within my heart,
And the hope so sweet and certain that again we'll never part.
A hundred thousand welcomes! how my heart is gushing o'er
With the love and joy and wonder thus to see your face once more.
How did I live without you these long long years of woe?

"...THE LOVE WITHIN MY HEART"

It seems as if 'twould kill me to be parted
from you now.
You'll never part me, darling, there's a
promise in your eye;
I may tend you while I'm living, you may
watch me when I die;
And if death but kindly lead me to the
blessed home on high,
What a hundred thousand welcomes will
await you in the sky.

They reached London on December 9, 1856. They celebrated Christmas as a family for the first time in five years. David played with his children almost as if they had never been apart.

He had come home hoping for a time of quiet rest. But he didn't know that in the sixteen years he had been away all of England had

CHRISTMAS AS A FAMILY

made him a hero. Because of the journals he had sent home, and because of various accounts written about him by traveling friends and other journalists in Africa, his home country had never forgotten him. David had written several reports of the slave trade and had sent them to magazines and newspapers. These reports did more than anything else to stir up the anger of the nation, and of the whole world, against the evil of slavery. In America, where the great Civil War was only a few years away, the nation was growing sharply divided because of that very curse, slavery. In Africa the war had already begun. British troops patroling the roads in the south had forced the slavers to move farther and farther into the north.

David had traveled over 11,000 miles of

THE SLAVERS HAD TO MOVE FARTHER NORTH...

African territory. In his travels he had always made careful recordings of sites of hills, rivers, and lakes, many of them unknown to anyone before him. He had written hundreds of pages describing the country—the geography, climate, peoples, and the products that could be produced and traded to bring wealth to a poor nation. His work, in fact, led to the development of new maps of much of Africa.

The scientific world was fascinated by David's careful observations. The Astronomer-Royal at Cape Town, Sir Thomas Maclear, said this of David's work:

"I never knew a man who, knowing scarcely anything of the method of making geographical observations, or laying down positions, became so soon an adept, that he could take the complete lunar observation, and altitudes

ASTRONOMER-ROYAL... SIR THOMAS MACLEAR

for time, within fifteen minutes."

He went on to say that Livingstone's work in mapping the course of the Zambezi River was "the finest specimen of sound geographical observation I ever met with. . . . I say, what that man has done is unprecedented . . . .You could go to any point across the entire continent, along Livingstone's track, and feel certain of your position."

David's life was now filled with speeches to universities, leçtures to scientific groups, meetings with government officials, invitations to social gatherings, and even an invitation from the Queen of England. He was made an honorary doctor of sciences by the University of Glasgow. And he had to write a book. A publisher named John Murray had convinced David that the world would want

DAVID'S LIFE WAS NOW FILLED WITH SPEECHES...LECTURES

to read of his travels in Africa. He agreed, but only because he believed that the book could serve his Lord.

He hated to sit hour after hour writing. His heart yearned for the open plains, the dark forests, and sleeping under the bright African stars.

His public life held no enjoyment, either. He wished only to stay home with his family.

A close friend of the Livingstone family would later write the following:

"Dr. Livingstone was very simple and unpretending, and used to be annoyed when he was made a lion of [fussed over]. Once a well-known gentleman, who was advertised to deliver a lecture next day, called on him to pump him for material. The Doctor sat rather quiet, and, without being rude, treated

...HIS HEART YEARNED FOR THE OPEN PLAINS

the gentleman to monosyllabic [one-syllable] answers. He could do that—could keep people at a distance when they wanted to make capital out of him. When the stranger had left, turning to my mother, [Livingstone] said, 'I'll tell *you* anything you like to ask.'

"He never liked to walk in the streets for fear of being mobbed [because of his being so popular]. Once he was mobbed in Regent Street, and did not know how he was to escape, till he saw a cab, and took refuge in it. For the same reason it was painful for him to go to church. Once, being anxious to go with us, my father persuaded him that, as the seat at the top of our pew was under the galley, he would not be seen. As soon as he entered, he held down his head, and kept it covered with his hands all the time, but the preacher some-

ONCE HE WAS MOBBED IN REGENT STREET

how caught sight of him, and rather unwisely, in his last prayer, adverted to him. This gave the people the knowledge that he was in the chapel, and after the service they came trooping toward him, even over the pews, in their anxiety to see him and shake hands."

David own letters to friends and family speak best for him:

"Nowhere have I ever appeared as anything else but a servant of God, who has simply followed the leadings of His hand. My views of what is *missionary* duty are not so contracted [limited] as those whose ideal is a dumpy sort of man with a Bible under his arm. I have labored in bricks and mortar, at the forge and carpenter's bench, as well as in preaching and medical practice. I feel that I am 'not my own.' I am serving Christ when

THE PRAYER... ADVERTED TO HIM!

shooting a buffalo for my men, or taking an astronomical observation, or writing to one of His children. . . ."

In December 1857 David was asked to speak at Oxford University. To the young men present he shared these thoughts.

"If you knew the satisfaction of performing such a duty [as missionaries], as well as the gratitude to God which the missionary must always feel, in being chosen for so noble, so sacred a calling, you would have no hesitation in embracing it. For my own part, I have never ceased to rejoice that God has appointed me to such an office. People talk of the sacrifice I have made in spending so much of my life in Africa. Can that be called a sacrifice which is simply paid back as a small part of a great debt owing to our God, which we can never

"... I HAVE NEVER CEASED TO REJOICE"

repay? . . .Say rather it is a privilege.

"I beg to direct your attention to Africa: I know that in a few years I shall be cut off in that country, which is now open; do not let it be shut again! I go back to Africa to try to make an open path for commerce and Christianity; do you carry out the work which I have begun. I leave it with you!"

He had come home with only the clothes on his back, He would return to Africa as one of the most famous men in England, in all the world.

In February of 1858 he had been given a formal commission as Her Majesty's Consul at Quilimane for the Eastern Coast and the independent districts in the interior, and commander of an expedition for exploring Eastern

... HE HAD BEEN GIVEN A FORMAL COMMISSION

and Central Africa.

His mission was plain, he knew. He wanted to find some healthy place, high in altitude, in Central Africa where missionaries could train natives to be teachers and preachers. He wanted to explore the jungles and rivers, to open up roads for trade—trade that would destroy slavery. Now he had the power of all of England at his command. David Livingstone's word would be law.

DAVID LIVINGSTONE'S WORD WOULD BE LAW!

WHERE WAS DAVID LIVINGSTONE?

9

In Darkness

Where was David Livingstone? All the world wanted to know. It was 1867, almost ten years since he had left England once again for Africa.

For several years the reports were sent to England, telling of his progress through Central Africa. But then one day all reports stopped. He seemed to have vanished. He had many enemies in Africa, to be sure. The Arab slave traders knew of David and they had stayed clear of him as he traveled northward. The slave traders knew that England had declared war on the slave trade, and that David carried the authority of the Queen. But now what had happened to him? Was he captured, or killed? Did he die in the brush from the African fever?

The world had learned of David's personal tragedy years earlier. His beloved Mary, who had traveled with him back to Africa, had become ill with the fever and had died.

Her death left David with a grief that he would carry for the rest of his life.

At Mary's death, David went north along the Rovuna River. He went almost aimlessly. He knew he must go on, to finish his work in this country. But now, though he still had his determination, his heart was gone. His heart, he felt, had been buried with Mary Livingstone in the town of Shupanca, where she had died.

Trudging along the trail by day, or sitting with his companions around a campfire by night, his thoughts had nowhere to go but onward. There would be no one waiting for him in Shupanca, in Kuruman, or in Mabotsa, the place of the

MARY... HAD DIED

marriage feast, where he and Mary had first lived. They would be reunited, he knew. But that reunion would not be for a long, long time. Mary was finally home, the home they never found together in this life, where they could rest from their wanderings and their work. When could *he* go home? He began to wonder now.

For now, there was only his work. On to the north. He wanted to reach Lake Nyassa. He believed that would be a good place to start an English colony. The land there was dry and healthy, he had heard, and the lake, which stretched north to south for over 400 miles, offered fresh water.

For for a while, there was news of David's journey north. They went up the Shire River in a steamer. They passed pineapple, orange, and lemon trees. Antelopes and elephants came out

WHEN COULD HE GO HOME ?

of the forests to the river to drink. Monkeys swung and chattered in the trees.

They came to Murchison Falls and could go no farther by water. They landed and marched on, coming to Lake Shirwa, about fifty miles south of the huge Lake Nyassa. They stayed here for a few days and then began the climb into the Manganja hills. On September 16, 1859, David's party, forty-two in all, came to the waters of beautiful Lake Nyassa, stretching away to the north beyond sight. David Livingstone was the first white man ever to see this lake.

But though there was beauty here, there was evil too. Arab sailing ships crossed Lake Nyassa, carrying newly captured slaves. Chained gangs of slaves were marched on paths along the shore.

David had an idea. A single British steamer carrying soldiers would stop the slave traffic on

... THE CLIMB INTO THE MANGANJA HILLS

the lake. British and American settlements on the shores would put an end to the slave trade in this whole region. He wrote letters home to England. Come and start a colony here, he wrote. Send missionaries, farmers, workers!

He would have to wait a long time for answers to his letters, he knew. Meanwhile, he had a promise to fulfill. He sailed down the Shire to Tette, where he met his Makololo friends. It was a joyful reunion. "We knew you would return for us," they said. And they went back the way they had come, to Linyanti.

When David returned once again to Tette, England's answer to his letters was waiting for him, a light steamer called the *Pioneer*. On board was a band of missionaries sent by Oxford and Cambridge universities, ready to go to work in the Shire Valley. England had said yes to

IT WAS A JOYFUL REUNION

David's requests, and here was the first group of workers.

They steamed up the Shire to Murchison Falls, then walked the rest of the way to Lake Nyassa. On the way they met a band of African slave drivers leading captive women and children. On seeing David, the slavers began shouting to one another and running off into the forest. Word was getting around: David Livingstone was out to stop the slave traffic.

The chained slaves cried and laughed and embraced their rescuers as David and his men sawed the forked sticks in two and unlocked the captives' bands. With the broken slave sticks, they made a fire and cooked breakfast for everyone. These freed slaves would become the first members of Lake Nyassa's mission church.

Livingstone then left these missionaries and

DAVID AND HIS MEN UNLOCKED THE CAPTIVES' BONDS

traveled north to the city of Zanzibar on the east coast. Here were the worst horrors of all. Slaves were sold in the marketplaces, like cattle, the buyers prodding their ribs and pulling open their mouths to look at their teeth. The day David arrived an Arab ship landed with 300 more slaves.

David was sick of the sounds and sights of Zanzibar. He rented a light ship and sailed south again. On foot and along narrow paths through grass taller than their heads they traveled, but all the villages they came to were empty. The huts were burned, the gardens uprooted, the people all gone—to the slavers.

They went on, to the north again. Their food ran low. After several weeks, all they had to eat was cornmeal soaked in goats' milk. Then one night the goats were stolen. On another night

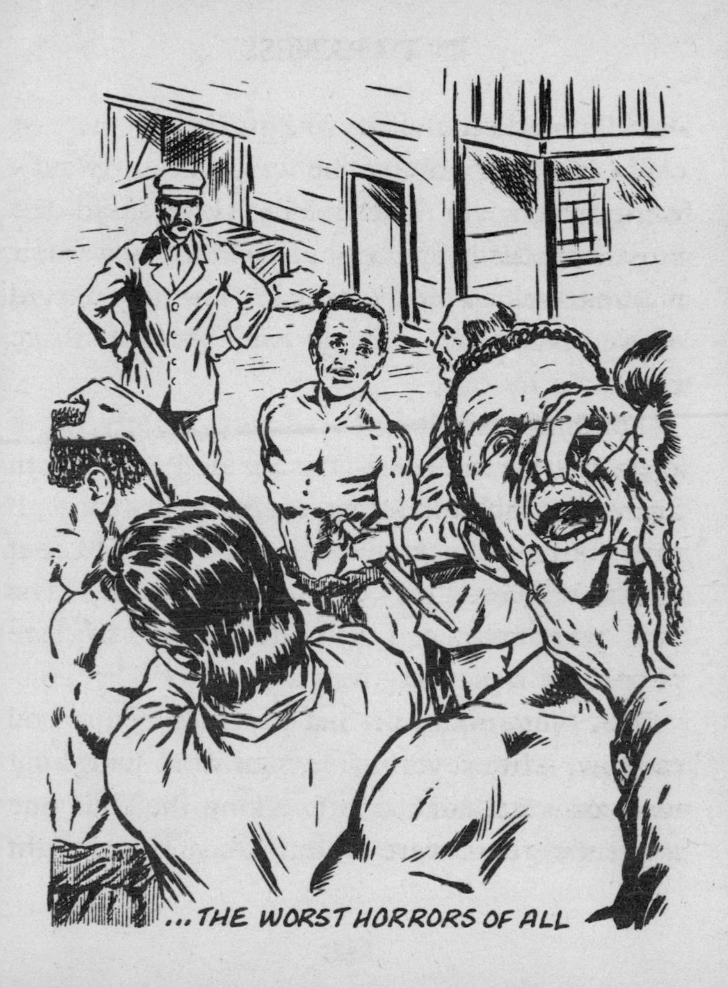

...THE WORST HORRORS OF ALL

David's medicine chest was stolen.

Without his medicine, he was constantly suffering from fever. Because the slavers had destroyed all the crops behind them as they went on, there was no food for the Livingstone party. With only the dry corn to eat, David lost his teeth, one by one.

They had to go on, There were no civilized settlements in this area. David needed to reach Ujiji, an Arab settlement on the east shore of Lake Tanganyika, about 300 miles west of Lake Nyassa. From there, he hoped to receive news from his country and his children. And to rest.

But there was a long way to go. David became so sick that finally he had to be carried, once again, in a litter. Only five men were with him now; the rest had run off. Along the trail the dangers were increasing day by day. The natives

...HE WAS CONSTANTLY SUFFERING FROM FEVER

who had not been captured were out seeking revenge. Any foreigner was their enemy, they believed, Although until now they were afraid to come near him, the Arab slave traders wanted David—dead.

Suddenly all were his enemies. None was his friend.

In England the reports came in: David Livingstone was lost. . . .or dead. The news reached America. Was it true? One man decided to find out.

WAS IT TRUE? ONE MAN DECIDED TO FIND OUT...

HE WAS AN AMERICAN...

10

The Last Journey

He was an American, that was clear. The American flag rode at the head of the procession. He wore light-colored clothes, a bush hat, and knee-high boots. Behind him came about 200 native porters wearing packs. Oxen pulled wagons loaded with canvas bundles.

They came up the street of Ujiji. The American looked slowly from right to left, scanning faces of blacks and Arabs. A white man now came out of a little house just up the street. He was skinny and bearded. His face and hands were almost as brown as those of the native men with him, who were dressed in English clothes. The white man's clothes hung loosely on his frame and were patched here and there but clean.

They met in the street. The American took off his hat and bowed slightly to the bearded man, Then he said, "Dr. Livingstone, I presume?"

When David had not been heard from for a long time, one man wanted to find out why. Gordon Bennett, publisher of the *New York Herald,* decided to find David. He would spend any amount necessary and would find him dead or alive. If alive, the *Herald* would be the first to report the news to the world. If dead, he would bring his bones home for burial and report that to the world.

Bennett sent a telegram on October 16, 1869, to Madrid, Spain, to one of his paper's traveling correspondents, Henry Morton Stanley. *Find Livingstone*, Bennett said—*dead or alive*. Take whatever you need, spend as much as you need, take as long as you need. *Just find him.*

"DR. LIVINGSTONE...I PRESUME?"

For some reason, Bennett sent Stanley on a roundabout journey: first to Constantinople (today Istanbul, Turkey), Palestine (Israel and the West Bank), and Egypt, then to India, before landing in Zanzibar in January 1871.

Stanley's expedition inland was massive. Almost 200 men in five caravans set out for Ujiji on Lake Tanganyika. From what he had learned, Stanley guessed that Ujiji was the last place David had been seen.

Stanley's party went slowly. Because of trouble on the roads—Arabs and native tribes were at war—Stanley had to turn far out of the way and travel south. The journey took from March to November.

Finally they reached Ujiji. Stanley later wrote of his meeting with David Livingstone:

"As I advanced slowly toward him, I noticed

STANLEY'S PARTY WENT SLOWLY

he was pale, looking wearied, had a gray beard, wore a bluish cap with a faded gold band round it, had on a red-sleeved waistcoat and a pair of gray tweed trousers. I would have run to him, only I was a coward in the presence of such a mob—would have embraced him, only he, being an Englishman, I did not know how he would receive me; so I did what cowardice and false pride suggested was the best thing —walked deliberately to him, took off my hat, and said, 'Dr. Livingstone, I presume?' 'Yes,' said he, with a kind smile, lifting his cap slightly. I replace my hat on my head, and he puts on his cap, and we both grasp hands, and then I say aloud—'I thank God, Doctor, I have been permitted to see you.' He answered, 'I feel thankful that I am here to welcome you.' "

David was indeed thankful. Stanley brought

"YES... SAID HE"

stores of food, clothes, sheets of copper, a tent, a boat, a bathtub, cooking pots, medicine, tools, books, paper, guns, and—most precious to David— letters. Stanley had brought a whole mailbag full. David ransacked the bag, digging through letters from friends and government officials, until he found what he was looking for. With tears in his eyes, he read the two letters from his children. (Somehow, Livingstone's mail had not gone in and out of Ujiji. He later learned that Arab slavers had held his mail so that he would die alone here, abandoned by the world.)

Stanley would stay here for over four months. The two would become close friends. They would sit and talk for hours each day. Of most value to David was news of the world. Stanley, too, was fascinated by all that David told him of his trav-

THEY WOULD SIT AND TALK FOR HOURS

els in Africa. He gave Stanley his journal, with all his personal and scientific notes, written from his arrival at Zanzibar on January 28, 1866, to February 20, 1872. He asked Stanley to take this back with him.

With good food and new medicine, David's health returned quickly. He had just got back from a long journey, he said, and had come into Ujiji almost dead. "You have brought me new life," he told Stanley, over and over.

Stanley came to love and respect David Livingstone. He would later write:

"You may take any point in Dr. Livingstone's character, and analyze it carefully, and I would challenge any man to find a fault in it. . . . His gentleness never forsakes him: his hopefulness never deserts him: No harassing anxieties, distraction of mind: long separation from home and

DAVID'S HEALTH RETURNED QUICKLY

kindred, can make him complain. . . .

"There is a good-natured *abandon* about Livingstone which was not lost on me. Whenever he began to laugh, there was a contagion about it that compelled me to imitate him. It was a laugh . . . of the whole man from head to heel. . . .

"Another thing that especially attracted my attention was his wonderful retentive memory. If we remember the many years he has spent in Africa, deprived of books, we may well think it an uncommon memory that can recite whole poems from Byron, Burns, Tennyson, Longfellow, Whittier, and Lowell . . . .

"His religion is not of the theoretical kind, but it is a constant, earnest, sincere practice. It is neither demonstrative nor loud, but manifests itself in a quiet, practical way, and is

"IT WAS A LAUGH... OF THE WHOLE MAN"

always at work. . . .

"From being thwarted and hated in every possible way upon his first arrival at Ujiji, he has, through his uniform kindness and mild, pleasant temper, won all hearts. I observed that mutual respect was paid to him. Even the Mohammedans never passed his house without calling to pay their compliments, and to say, 'The blessing of God rest on you.' Each Sunday morning he gathers his little flock around him, and reads prayers and a chapter from the Bible, in a natural, unaffected, and sincere tone; and afterward delivers a short address in the Kisqwahili language, about the subject read to them, which is listened to with evident interest and attention."

The day finally came for Henry Stanley to leave. "March 14th—We had a sad breakfast

"HE HAS ... THROUGH HIS KINDNESS... WON ALL HEARTS"

together. I could not eat, my heart was too full; neither did my companion seem to have an appetite. We found something to do which kept us together longer. At eight o'clock I was not gone, and I had thought to have been off at five A.M. . . . We walked side by side; the men lifted their voices in a song. I took long looks at Livingstone to impress his features thoroughly on my memory. . . . 'Now, my dear Doctor, the best friends must part. You have come far enough; let me beg of you to turn back.' 'Well,' Livingstone replied, 'I will say this to you: You have done what few men could do—far better than some great travelers I know. And I am grateful to you for what you have done for me. God guide you safe have, and bless you, my friend.'—'And may God bring you safe back to us all, my dear friend. Fare-

"GOD... BLESS YOU... MY FRIEND"

well!'—'Farewell!' "

"Susi, bring my watch," came the faint voice from inside the hut. Susi, David's trusted native friend for many years, went in and gently laid the watch in his palm.

They had just come to this village, called Ilala. They had been traveling for weeks. David had wanted to make one more journey, this one to find the great river called Luapula that he had heard many rumors about. This river, it was said, was the source of the Nile River. No one had ever found the source of the Nile.

But here they had to stop. David was so weak with a new attack of the fever that he could not go on. He lay now in the cool darkness of the hut, too weak even to lift his arm. Susi sat by his friend. Night came. Just after eleven o'clock,

SUSI SAT BY HIS FRIEND

Livingstone spoke again.

"Is this the Luapula?"

"No," Susi said softly. "We are in Chitambo's village near the Molilamo."

"How many days is it to the Luapula?"

"I think it is three days, Master."

David was silent now. Susi waited until his master was asleep, then went to his own hut.

Just before dawn, Susi was awakened. "Come to Bwana [master]," said the boy. "I am afraid."

Susi and three others went quickly to David's hut. His candle had burned low. In its dim, flickering light, the four men saw the still form of their master and friend kneeling by his bed, his head buried in his hands on his pillow.

The men waited, silent, in the doorway. They never disturbed their master while he was praying. But how did he find the strength to get out

HOW DID HE FIND THE STRENGTH TO GET OUT OF BED?

of bed and kneel? Hours earlier, he could barely talk.

They waited and waited. David's candle went out. Susi lit another and went softly to David and touched his cheek. Then the tears that he had been holding back till now streamed down his face. His master's cheek was cold.

David Livingstone was home.

In Westminster Abbey in London where David Livingstone is buried, you can find a headstone with the following words.

> Brought by faithful hands over land and over sea, Here Rests DAVID LIVINGSTONE, Missionary Traveler, Philanthropist. Born March 19, 1813, At Blantyre, Lanarkshire. Died May 4th, 1873, At

DAVID LIVINGSTONE WAS HOME !

Chitambo's Village, Ilala. For thirty years his life was spent in an unwearied effort to evangelize the native races, to explore the undiscovered secrets, And abolish the desolating slave-trade of Central Africa, where, with his last words, he wrote: "All I can say in my solitude is, May Heaven's rich blessing come down on every one—American, English, Turk—who will help to heal the open sore of the world."